Diva Duck Dreams

BY Janice Levy

ILLUSTRATED BY
Colleen Madden

magic
wagon

visit us at www.abdopublishing.com

Published by Magic Wagon, a division of the ABDO Group, PO Box 398166,
Minneapolis, MN 55439. Copyright © 2013 by Abdo Consulting Group, Inc.
International copyrights reserved in all countries. All rights reserved. No part of this
book may be reproduced in any form without written permission from the publisher.

Looking Glass Library™ is a trademark and logo of Magic Wagon.

Printed in the United States of America, North Mankato, Minnesota.
052012
092012
 This book contains at least 10% recycled materials.

Written by Janice Levy
Illustrations by Colleen Madden
Edited by Stephanie Hedlund and Rochelle Baltzer
Cover and interior design by Jaime Lint

Library of Congress Cataloging-in-Publication Data

Levy, Janice.
  Diva Duck dreams / by Janice Levy ; illustrated by Colleen Madden.
      p. cm. – (Diva Duck)
  Summary: Diva Duck dreams of becoming famous as a singer.
  ISBN 978-1-61641-886-1
  1. Ducks–Juvenile fiction. 2. Animals–Juvenile fiction. 3. Fame–Juvenile fiction.
(1. Ducks–Fiction. 2. Animals–Fiction. 3. Fame–Fiction.) I. Madden, Colleen M., ill. II. Title.
  PZ7.L5832Dim 2012
  (E)–dc23
                                   2011051958

Diva did all the duck stuff, but her feathers weren't in it.

Diva had **dreams**.

"I am destined for greatness," she said.

"I can feel it in my webbing."

"Feel **this**," said the cow,
swishing her tail.

"Go **lay** an egg," cackled one of the hens.

Diva stuck her beak in the air.
"One day you'll read all about me.
My name will be in lights."

"Yeah, on a **dinner menu**," snorted the pig.

"Just **whoooooo**
do you think you are?"
hooted the owl.

"I am Diva Duck, destined
for greatness," Diva sniffed.
She waddled by, wiggling her butt.

Diva lay on her back and watched the clouds change shape. She dreamed of life beyond the farm. She waited for her magic moment.

One day, the farmer had a party.
Loud music **blasted** through speakers.

Diva felt a tingling
in her wings.

Her beak twitched.

Her hips swiveled.

Her butt went boom-ducka-boom.

She spun on her head.

She flipped and dipped.

The duck was poppin'.

Diva ducked into the DJ's booth. She scratched records and mixed the beats.

The animals tumbled into a mosh pit.
"Diva!" the crowd exploded.
"Diva Duck!"

"You talkin' to ME?"
she quacked.

A star was born!

Videos flooded the Internet.

Reporters dropped from helicopters.

Paparazzi hid in the bushes.

Designers **begged** Diva to wear their latest creations.

Everyone wanted a piece of duck.

Diva left the pond. She traveled around the world, opening up new dance clubs.

The pig went as her personal chef.
The cow was her yoga instructor.
The sheep was her hairstylist.
And the chickens were in the chorus line.

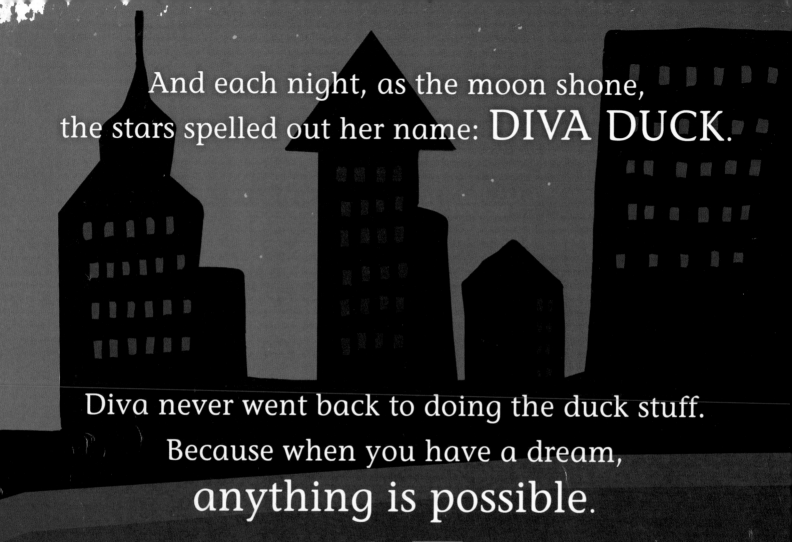

And each night, as the moon shone,
the stars spelled out her name: DIVA DUCK.

Diva never went back to doing the duck stuff.
Because when you have a dream,
anything is possible.

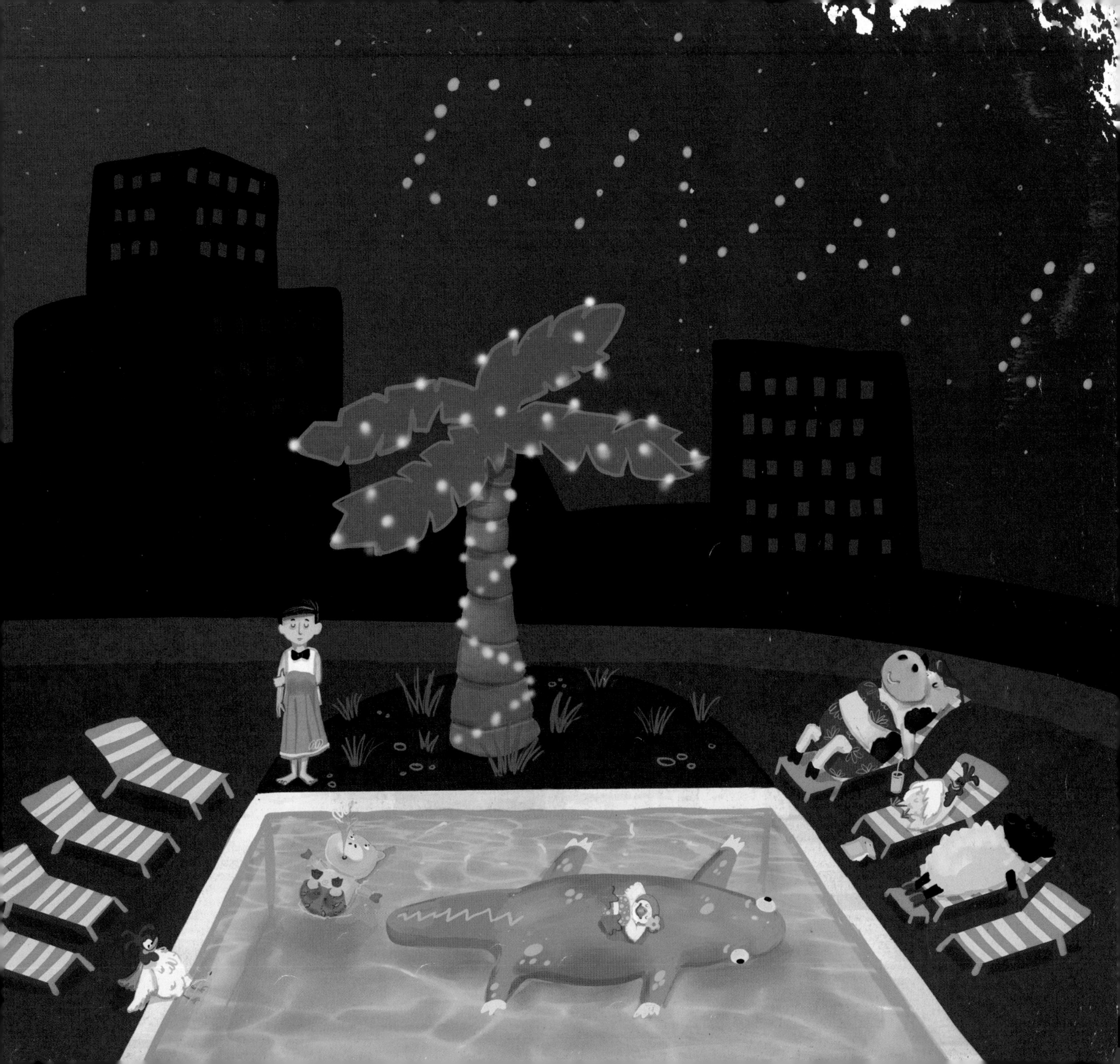

Diva Duck

★ Many of the farm animals didn't believe in Diva Duck. What were some of the things they said she couldn't do?

★ Diva Duck had big dreams and believed in herself. What is one of your dreams?

About the Author: Janice Levy is the author of numerous award-winning children's books. Topics include bullying, multiculturalism, foster care, intergenerational relationships, and family values. She teaches creative writing at Hofstra University. Her adult fiction is widely published in magazines and anthologies.

About the Illustrator: Colleen Madden is an illustrator, mom, kickboxer, ukulele strummer, and honorary frog. She loves to draw for kids (and kids at heart!) and make people giggle. Diva Duck is her fourth series of children's books. She is currently writing her own titles as author/illustrator, which will all be very silly books.